OLD WOODY
BUILDS A HOUSE

CANDLE
BOOKS

'My house is very old,' said Old Woody one day. 'I shall build a much better house for me and my cat Filbert. And I'll do it properly – not like Selwyn Slapdash.'

Selwyn Slapdash had seen just the place where he wanted to live. It was on a stretch of sand by the sea. As soon as he saw it, Selwyn said: 'I'm going to build my house right here!'

First Selwyn Slapdash decided how big his house was to be. It didn't need to be very big, because he lived all by himself.

Next Selwyn Slapdash bought lots of planks of wood and a big box of nails. Then he set to work building his new house. Selwyn hammered and sawed all day – right until it was time to go to bed.

Selwyn Slapdash wouldn't let anybody help him.
'I can do it all myself,' he said.
But sometimes things went wrong. Once he hit
his thumb with the hammer. That really hurt!

Selwyn worked day after day. After all the hammering was done, he started painting.
At last everything was finished. He stood back to admire his work.
'Didn't I do well!' said Selwyn Slapdash.

But that very evening it started to rain. And it wasn't just a little shower. It rained and rained. And there was thunder and lightning too! Selwyn Slapdash was worried. He rushed out of his new front door. Whatever was happening to his house?

The sea had grown very wild, and great waves were crashing against the house. Gales were blowing the roof off. But even worse – the sand under Selwyn's house was all washing away. Crrrrash!! Suddenly Selwyn's house collapsed.

So Old Woody planned his house very carefully.
'I shall build my house in a really safe place,' he
said. 'It must stand quite firm.'

The very next day Old Woody started to build his new house.

Filbert the cat watched every move he made.

First Old Woody sawed up some very thick planks of wood. Then he fixed the planks into the ground. They would form the foundations for his house.

Old Woody knew that foundations must be very firm. If a house is built on good foundations, it doesn't just collapse.

Old Woody stood back to admire his handiwork.
His house looked safe and strong. He was
very pleased. Now all he had to do was put on
the roof.

There! At last it was all finished. It had been a very big job. Now, with a little help from Filbert the cat, Old Woody put away his tools.

Then Woody took a rest.
He could live safe and sound in his new house.
Whatever happened, his home would remain
standing.

Old Woody built his house on rock.
A flood could come – or a great storm – but Old Woody's house would stand firm, because it was built properly.

This story about Old Woody is similar to a story
Jesus told about two men who each built a house.
You can read it in your Bible in Luke 6:46-49.
Jesus said, 'Trust in me, and do as I tell you. Then
you will be as strong and safe as a house built on
rock.'